It's great outdoors

written and illustrated by John Light

Published by Child's Play (International) Ltd
Swindon   **Bologna**   **New York**
© M. Twinn 1989   ISBN 0-85953-338-7   Printed in Singapore
Library of Congress Catalogue Number 90-34353
This impression 1992

Katherine, Mark and Roger like being out in the garden.

When Mum decided to have a new bathtub,
Dad helped the plumber to slide the old one downstairs.

Mark said, "I've got a spare hole
we could put that bath in...

... to make a pond."

"Be careful you don't fall in,"
warned Dad when they finished.

But when it became overgrown...

... Dad forgot it was there.

Mum told Dad it was time he got rid of some old clothes ...

But he didn't want to throw them away...

... so he hid them in the shed.

Later, he used them to make a scarecrow.

That night, the boys decided to camp in the garden.

They were soon snug in their tent.

Suddenly, they heard a noise.
"It's the scarecroak," cried Roger.

But when Mark looked out,
he saw it was just a green frog from the pond.

The next night, Dad slept out, too.
His feet slept right out.

Katherine didn't set her tent up quite right.

Uncle Richard said he would show Mark
what real camping was like. They took lots of things.

Even so, Uncle Richard had to call in for extra supplies.

They found a beautiful camp site in the great outdoors . . .

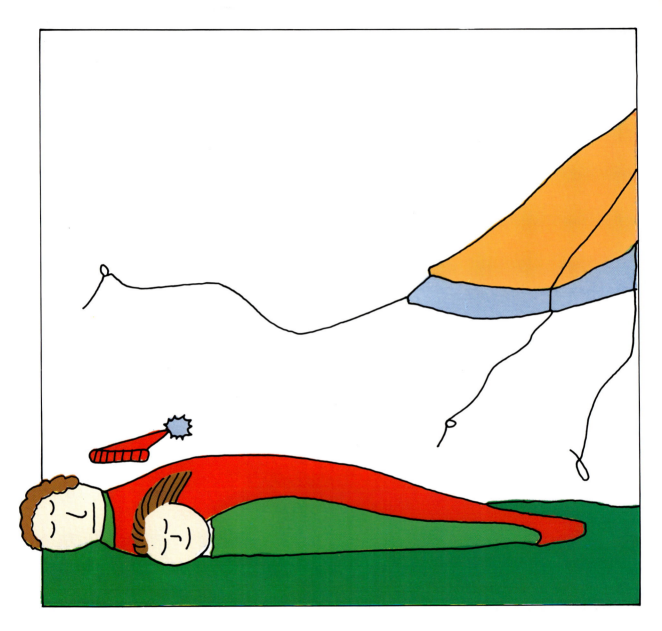

... where they could enjoy the fresh air.

When they arrived home, Mark told Roger all about it.

Roger decided it was safer camping indoors.